PaRragon

Bath • New York • Singapore • Hong Kong • Cologne • Delhi
Melbourne • Amsterdam • Johannesburg • Auckland • Shenzhen

First published by Parragon in 2012

Parragon
Queen Street House
4 Queen Street
Bath BA1 1HE, UK
www.parragon.com

Based on the screenplay by Elise Allen. Illustrated by Ulkutay Design Group
Special thanks to Sarah Buzby, Vicki Jaeger, Dana Koplik, Ann McNeill, Emily Kelly, Sharon Woloszyk, Julia Phelps,
Tanya Mann, Rob Hudnut, David Wiebe, Tiffany J. Shuttleworth, Gabrielle Miles,
Rainmaker Entertainment, Walter P. Martishius, Carla Alford, Rita Lichtwardt and Kathy Berry

ISBN 978-1-4454-7235-5

Printed in China

Surfing superstars Merliah and Kylie both qualify for the World Championship in Australia! Who will be crowned Queen of the Waves?

Merliah uses her special necklace to transform into a mermaid and tell her mum, Calissa the queen of Oceana.

During the first heat, Merliah's
impressive style and grace in the whirling
water is matched by Kylie's risky spins.

A final wicked kick-flip from Kylie forces
Merliah to do a handstand on her board
before falling into a watery wipeout.

Although Kylie wins the heat,
everyone is buzzing about Merliah.
She always manages to be more popular than Kylie!

That evening, a rainbow fish called Alistair swims up to Kylie and tells her that he knows how to beat Merliah. Kylie is super shocked that a fish is talking to her, but is desperate to know what she can do to be Queen of the Waves.

The fish tells Kylie that Merliah has a magical necklace, which turns her into a mermaid. To find out how, she has to take the necklace from Merliah's hoodie. Kylie jumps into action.

Kylie rushes back to Alistair and he encourages her to put the necklace on and get in the water. Kylie whispers that she wishes to become a mermaid and a wonderful, sparkly magic glow changes her legs into a beautiful tail – incredible!

Telling her she will get all the answers she wants if she follows him, the mystery fish leads Kylie down into the ocean depths.

In a deep trench at the bottom of the seabed, a whirlpool glistens in the dark.
Kylie falls into the whirlpool and Calissa's evil sister is released! She's escaped her prison just in time to takeover the Changing of the Tides ceremony and capture the power of Merillia. The ocean will finally be hers!
No one sees a baby sealion hiding by a rock...

Merliah and her friends are searching for her necklace on the beach. Suddenly Snouts appears and tells Merliah what happened to Kylie.

Merliah and Snouts find Kylie's whirlpool and promise to get her out.

Merliah ties one end of a piece of strong seaweed around her ankle and the other end to a big rock, and leaps in. Amazingly, Kylie is released and quickly swims to safer water.

Oops! Kylie and Snouts soon realize that Merliah is trapped in Kylie's place! Merliah tries to climb up the seaweed but the current is too strong. Kylie grabs the seaweed and pulls with all her strength, telling Merliah that the Queen of the Waves never gives up. Snouts joins in and Merliah bursts out of the whirlpool.

Kylie vows to help Merliah stop Eris and save the ocean.

Calissa and Zuma arrive at the grand city of Aquellia, where everything is being done to get the throne ready for the Changing of the Tides ceremony. Mermaids from around the world have gathered and their ambassadors greet her warmly.

Each ambassador presents a special gem to the ancient mermaid throne and puts it in position for the ceremony.

Suddenly a laugh is heard in the shadows....

Eris and her gang of stargazers attack! The sisters dodge and block each other's magical bolts, but it is Eris who succeeds in zapping her sister. A worst-nightmare spell wraps Calissa's tail with a magical weight. She struggles, but her heavy tail pulls her down, until she sinks out of sight!

The ambassadors do their best to try to stop Eris and defend the throne. Unfortunately the wicked mermaid has other ideas. With help from her gang of stargazers, she blasts the mermaids with her worst-nightmare spells before locking them in a magical cage.

Zuma zips to Merliah and Kylie and shows them where Calissa is.

  The group try again and again to pull Calissa up, but Eris' spell has made her tail too heavy. Merliah decides that she must take her mother's place in the ceremony and save Oceana herself, even though it means that she might have a tail forever.

Merliah, Kylie, Snouts and Zuma swim to the throne and hide before Eris and her gang of stargazers spot them.

Kylie notices the thick seaweed that's around them and makes a joke about using it as a lasso. Merliah thinks it's a great idea!

The stargazers' eyes are on top of their heads, so Merliah, Kylie, Zuma and Snouts keep below them to remain unnoticed as they work quickly to lasso the strong seaweed around their big tails. The other end of each piece of seaweed is tied to a big rock.

There are just two stargazers still free when the midday sun breaks into the water, signalling the start of the Changing of the Tides ceremony!

Eris can't wait for the ceremony to
begin – soon she will be given the power of
Merillia and will rule all of Oceana.

Merliah and Kylie take a deep breath then move
sharply and swiftly. In a flash they slip the seaweed ropes
into the stargazers' mouths and jump on their backs, so they
can control the mighty fish with reins.

Eris is furious and throws angry magic bolts at the approaching
stargazers, who rear up and roar.

Merliah and Kylie are determined to defeat Eris and zoom closer. Kylie manages to steer her stargazer close enough to make Eris fall from the throne!

As she falls, Eris sends more magical bolts towards the special gems to stop the ceremony.

Merliah swims into place but nothing happens. Eris laughs evilly and tells Merliah that because she hasn't got a tail she can't activate the throne. If there's no transformation, there's no Merillia and the life force of the ocean will be lost. Merliah doesn't know what to do. Eris must perform the ceremony or the ocean will die!

Kylie acts quickly. Taking off her necklace, Kylie becomes a girl again and holds her breath as she places the necklace around Merliah's head.

Merliah wishes to become a mermaid. Will she switch in time?

In a bubbly whoosh of sparkly magic, Merliah is bathed in light and transformed into the beautiful mer-princess she was born to be, with the power to create Merillia.

The Changing of the Tides ceremony is complete and Oceana is saved! Merliah's tail and outfit are even more gorgeous than before and her hair is long and beautiful.

Eris tries to cast a final worst-nightmare spell at the princess, but the colourful swirling light blasts it right back at her and Eris falls into a patch of prickly kelp. Ouch!

As soon as the sensational light fades, Merliah rushes to Kylie's side. Her friend needs her necklace to breathe under water!

Tired and weak, Kylie manages to gurgle her wish to become a mermaid....

In a few magical moments, Kylie is changed into a mermaid again. Merliah and Kylie hug happily – they did it!

Calissa and the ambassadors thank Merliah and Kylie for saving them.

Eris realizes her final worst-nightmare spell came true, but on herself – she now has legs!

Merliah tells Kylie that since she can't surf with a tail, Kylie will need to win the surfing World Championship for both of them. Kylie doesn't care about the competition any more, but Merliah and Calissa persuade her that there is still time to get to the beach and take part.

Everyone says goodbye to their new friends and Calissa leads the way to the World Championship!

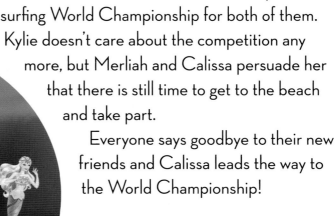

At the surface, Kylie wishes to become a human and happily accepts when Calissa asks her to be an ambassador for Oceana.

Merliah wishes she could have her legs back to surf in the competition and incredibly her legs return! The ceremony transformed her into her fullest self, which is being both a mermaid and a human. Calissa wishes the delighted girls good luck and Merliah and Kylie swim to shore.

The surfers are just in time for the biggest waves of the tournament. Merliah and Kylie ride a monster break, laughing as they playfully try to out trick each other. Who will tame the wild water?

Suddenly, Merliah sees Merillia glistening off her board and floating out into the ocean. It spins beautifully as she turns and twists, surfing for pure pleasure.

A thrilled Merliah tells Kylie to take the World Championship; she's enjoying just playing in the water. Kylie smiles at her friend and surfs to a glorious finish with a mega flip.

On shore, the photographers are super excited – Kylie and Merliah put on an amazing performance. Everyone wants to know about Kylie's brilliant moves!

Kylie is so happy to be World Champion, but she makes sure she shares her moment with Merliah. The girls lift the trophy and are surrounded by cheering friends.